J.J. Dempsy

The Coroner's Court

Anatiposi

J.J. Dempsy

The Coroner's Court

Reprint of the original.

1st Edition 2023 | ISBN: 978-3-38230-542-0

Anatiposi Verlag is an imprint of Outlook Verlagsgesellschaft mbH.

Verlag (Publisher): Outlook Verlag GmbH, Zeilweg 44, 60439 Frankfurt, Deutschland
Vertretungsberechtigt (Authorized to represent): E. Roepke, Zeilweg 44, 60439 Frankfurt, Deutschland
Druck (Print): Books on Demand GmbH, In de Tarpen 42, 22848 Norderstedt, Deutschland

THE

CORONER'S COURT,

Its Uses and Abuses;

WITH SUGGESTIONS FOR REFORM.

BY

J. J. DEMPSY,

A MEMBER OF THE METROPOLITAN PRESS, AND AUTHOR OF A PAMPHLET
ON THE LONDON MAIN DRAINAGE.

ADDRESSED TO THE
LEGISLATURE AND THE PEOPLE OF THE UNITED KINGDOM;

AND DEDICATED TO
THE RIGHT HON. LORD BROUGHAM,
AND THE MEMBERS OF THE LAW AMENDMENT SOCIETY.

SECOND EDITION.

WITH PREFATORY ADDRESS TO LORD BROUGHAM,

AND APPENDIX,
CONTAINING SKETCH OF PROPOSED NEW BILL, ETC.

Per varios casus, per tot discrimina rerum
Tendimus——

LONDON:
HATTON AND CO., 99, CHANCERY-LANE.
1859.

Price One Shilling.

ALEX. MACINTOSH,
PRINTER,
GREAT NEW-STREET, LONDON.

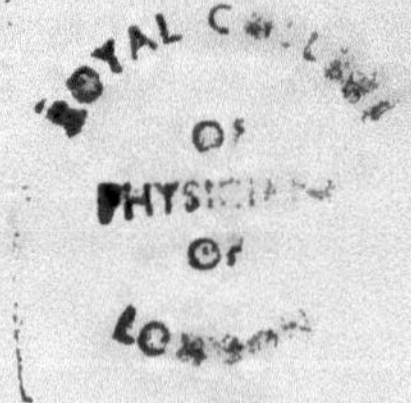

PREFACE TO SECOND EDITION.

TO THE RIGHT HON. LORD BROUGHAM.

My Lord,

It is exceedingly gratifying, in issuing a second edition at so early a period, to observe that the public have embraced the important subject thus brought under their attention in so warm a spirit. Indeed, I felt, *in limine*, before thus publicly broaching the question, that it only required a clear and concise statement of facts to arouse the public mind; and now, with your Lordship's powerful support and invaluable assistance, —without presuming too much on your Lordship's time—and that of the members of the learned and active Society of which your Lordship is President, I can look forward with confidence to an early period when such a reform will be effected through Parliament as will place the Coroner's Court in its independent and proper position. Thus, all unseemly jarring between coroners, magistrates, and police jurisdiction, will be prevented. At the same time justice will be acceded to one of the most ancient and important institutions the country possesses; and, by strengthening its power, and extending to the Court a searching and wholesome system of sanatory surveillance, inestimable benefits, so far as the health and lives of the community at large are concerned, will accrue to the State, and an ever-watchful protection be thrown around the homes of all, more especially the working and poorer classes, who, but for such an institution, might become the victims, at some future period, of a callous, negligent, and cruel Administration.

Since the first issue of the subjoined treatise some very important steps have been taken towards completing the great object aimed at, viz., the settlement of the Coroners' question, on a just, substantial, and equitable basis. At the Social Science Congress held at Liverpool I had the honour, through the kindness of your Lordship, of bringing the subject before that assembly in a paper written specially for the occasion, and which was read in the Jurisprudence and Amendment of the Law Department. I was unfortunately absent on that occasion; but I am informed that a discussion ensued which was of a very satisfactory character; and, considering the leading position in the Legislative Assembly of many of those who took an active part in the proceedings of the Congress, much ultimate good may be expected from their support.

Subsequently a Meeting of the Law Amendment Society was called, to consider the question. On that occasion your Lordship presided, and the paper read at Liverpool, which, through arriving late, had unfortunately to be thrown out of the printed transactions of the Congress, was presented with additions, to the Meeting. I also read the heads of a proposed measure that I had concocted to meet the requirements of the case; and after some discussion, a Committee was appointed to consider the whole subject, and that Committee is now sitting.

Some extracts from the paper alluded to, and a sketch of the proposed consolidated measure, form a part of the Appendix to this second edition.

A subject of much importance as connected with the Coroners' question, has already been brought before Parliament. That is with respect to granting power to Coroners to bail in charges of manslaughter; and your Lordship, I think, will agree, that, as a matter of justice, this should be at once acceded to, without waiting for the passing of any special Coroners' Bill.

In the paper presented to the Law Amendment Society, I have particularly alluded to the present state of the law ruling charges of infanticide and concealment of birth. I propose to prosecute more searchingly and severely for concealment of birth, in order to check the fearful crime of infanticide— a crime which has unhappily swollen into a magnitude awful to contemplate; owing, as I consider, to a great extent the guilty in many such cases escaping punishment on mere legal technicalities, and frequently through juries being averse to the infliction of capital punishment for a crime where human frailty and another's villany have been the chief causes of the wretched accused's fallen position. Inflict, as I propose, a severe punishment, apart from death, for concealment of birth—not simply for concealment of the body, which is really the case under existing circumstances, and this shocking social evil, I doubt not, will be in a great measure at once checked, if not entirely eradicated.

I then propose to abolish the absurd inquiry into the state of mind of a person who has committed suicide, and thus entirely erase from the statute book that remnant of barbarism found in verdicts of *felo de se*. Investigations in cases of supposed suicide under the new law would be to prove whether the act was that of the deceased or another. It would come under the head of investigations in deaths from violence, and the jury would only be called upon to say how and by whom the fatal violence was caused. I think your Lordship will fully concur with me, that jurymen might as well endeavour to unravel the mysteries of eternity, as the state of the mind of a deceased fellow-creature, and their being frequently compelled, according to the existing state of the law, to return verdicts of *felo de se*, is a barbarous and cruel alternative, such a proceeding being no punishment on the dead, but an exceedingly severe one on the living, in the persons of the suicide's relatives and friends.

I strongly maintain, my Lord, that the Coroner's Court should be intrusted with the sanatory welfare of the country; and that Coroners, in fact, should be regarded as chief officers of health. Powers should be given to hold investigations in all sanatory matters, and to issue orders for the abatement of dangerous nuisances. The health of the whole country is concerned, and what more impartial and observant officer could there be appointed for such purpose than the Coroner, who is constantly in the midst of disease, and by practical, if not professional experience, sees the real causes of a devastating epidemic, and, as far as human foresight goes, can direct the application of proper and effectual remedies. Thus, while external causes of disease might be prevented, the apothecary and chemist should be checked in the indiscriminate sale of poisons and the dispensing of *impure drugs and compounds*, and those who adulterate the common necessaries of life could be dealt with in the same manner. These are all matters affecting the vital existence of the people, and who are better able to consider them than the people themselves through their own representative Court—the Coroner's?

It may be urged that the imposition of such extra duties would overburden the Coroner; but it should be borne in mind that the special inquiries alluded to would be few and far between. They would not be of daily, or even monthly, occurrence, after a proper system of sanatory *régime* had been established, and, in fact, a few searching investigations and prosecutions would speedily be the means of abating the evils complained of, and checking a nefarious system.

The present mode of voting for Coroners in counties is, I consider, most objectionable, through the voting being confined to the freeholders, and owing to the whole county being called upon to vote when only one division is concerned. I conceive every one has a vital interest in matters relating to the public health, and why not, therefore, allow every person duly registered on the Parliamentary lists to vote in the election of Coroner? As to the voting in divisions, that is, the voting being confined to those residing in the district over which the Coroner elected is to have charge, the period for the election, now extended to ten or fourteen days, could be limited by such division to two or three.

I have, my Lord, in the Bill particularly alluded to public prosecutors and public analytical officers. Every one appears to have agreed upon the desirability and importance of the appointment of public prosecutors, and, as regards public analytical officers, I believe the appointment of such officers, in these days of secret poisoning and adulteration, is as much called for. Dr. Farr, the Registrar-General, in his observations on Coroners' inquests, remarks:—"Poisoning is not mentioned in the Act of Edward; but poisoning is now, unhappily, a common cause of death. Poisons are the most insidious instruments which assassins can employ, and they were evidently little known in England before the Reformation; yet the first English legislators directed inquests to be held on the body of a person dying suddenly, because death might possibly even then be the result of secret violence. Persons slain generally die suddenly; hence, it was made the rule to hold inquests in cases of sudden death.

Such was the wise provision of the law." Now, the fact is, that very few medical men can perform a searching analytical examination. This is only to be arrived at after years spent in analytical researches and studies, and therefore when a good analysis is required, such eminent analysts as Dr. Taylor, Professor Herapath, and Mr. Rodgers have to be resorted to. No provision is made in law for this extra evidence, and Coroners, I am informed, have had, frequently through the magistrate's refusing to pay such fees, to defray them themselves. Calmly and dispassionately considering these arguments, I think there are very few but will agree with the necessity of appointing these officers. The public prosecutor and the public analytical officer must, of necessity, become adjuncts to our modern criminal jurisdiction. As to the question of extra expense, if such sordid ideas are to be commingled with the administration of truth and justice, this would be trifling, as one public prosecutor or analytical officer could have charge over several districts, their advice and assistance, at least so far as the analytical officer was concerned, being only required on notable and special occasions.

There are many other matters of detail connected with this question which I will not now broach, as they can be better dealt with in Committee, and, above all, I trust the equity of pensioning Coroners who " perform their arduous duty till old age and infirmities overtake them, and are then obliged to retire without any provision, after having devoted the time and energies of a whole life to the public service," will be duly considered.

I fear, my Lord, that I may have, as it is, in these prefatory observations, encroached too much upon your valuable time; but I feel certain that I need only throw myself upon your Lordship's kind indulgence when I say that the vastness of the important question involved, and a sense of public duty, have alone actuated my humble efforts.

"Nil actum reputans si quid superesset agendum."

I remain,

My Lord,

Your obedient Servant,

J. J. DEMPSY.

34, Essex-street, Middle Temple,
April, 1859.

CORONERS' COURTS.

For years past the proceedings as conducted in the Coroners' Courts throughout those districts of the United Kingdom where the office possesses its prerogative, and the necessity for the formation of such a tribunal in Scotland, have attracted marked attention amongst all classes of the community; the more so, it might be added, within the last nine or ten years, when, through the instrumentality of this ancient and important institution, the most serious crimes in the shape of secret poisoning that ever tarnished England's social system have been brought to light, and the guilty, in accordance with the stringent, but, at the same time, just and salutary, laws of the land, made to expiate their atrocious crimes.

Through the medium of the Court, cases of gross cruelty, at the hands of callous, inhuman officials, have been at the same time exposed; and if, owing to the want of a more rigorous code, the morally guilty have not met with that legal punishment due to their offences, yet they have received that moral castigation before the eyes of an indignant public which on many occasions must have proved more searching and severe than the infliction of penal punishment.

The necessity, usefulness, and power of such a Court as that of the Coroner have been from time to time widely discussed, and narrow and partial is the mind that denies its national importance and dignity.

Since the introduction of the new police system, and the appointment of stipendiary magistrates, the necessity for the continuance of the Crown officers'* jurisdiction has been often called in question, and much contention and unseemly legal strife have arisen from time to time between the representatives of the magisterial bench and those of the Coroner's Court, in the discharge of their respective duties, originating in the want of a better system of management, and an illiberal definition of the duties of the two Courts.

As such painful scenes have arisen through conflicting authority, it is evident the present very anomalous state of the law ruling both Courts requires amendment. Such contentious spirit having been only lately revived in one of the most populous and important districts of the metropolis (*i. e.,* the western division of the county of Middlesex), where a Coroner's Jury refused to record a verdict in a case of alleged murder; and similar proceedings having been adopted a short time previously, in another

* Coroner, from *corona,* a crown.

county, where in both cases the Juries urged that their duties had been seriously and unnecessarily interfered with by the magistrates, it is high time, for the proper administration of justice, and the honour of England's sapient laws, that a better understanding should arise, and such jarring proceedings be in future prevented.

It becomes, therefore, a most important inquiry whether, while enforcing the due administration of affairs in both Courts, the power and dignity of the Coroner's Court cannot be strengthened and upheld, and its usefulness carried into those districts where, as in Scotland, there exists at the present period no such tribunal.

Under such circumstances, as one who has taken a deep interest in the subject, and who, as a representative of the public press, has had much experience therein, the writer of this short address desires to expose the existing evils, and, in laying down certain recommendations, trusts, while pointing out the bane, in a few brief suggestions to supply the antidote by those remedies which appear feasible, and which, in fact, carried out, would effect an entire reform on the subject.

No reasonable person can deny that the Coroner's Court is one of the oldest and most useful existing, dating, as its stability does, from the reign of Alfred the Great, whose name as a legislator is alone sufficient to stamp it with importance and dignity.

The Coroner's Court has, indeed, an excellent and overpowering argument in its favour at the outset, considering that the office owes its existence to a monarch the sapiency of whose laws has never been questioned, and whose whole aim and object in their formation were his country's welfare, his country's happiness.

Dating the authority of the Coroner's Court from this wise and excellent monarch, without further comment upon the wisdom and discretion of its origin, we come down to the present period, and, analysing its uses and its abuses, consider the best means of placing it in such a position that it shall prove one of the most important branches of our criminal legislature and one of the greatest boons ever annexed to our social system.

Reviewing impartially the important duties attached to this office, there cannot be a member of the community who doubts its usefulness, or who cannot see the great good that must accrue to the State, both in a pecuniary and a social point of view, by its being carried out in a strictly legal and searching manner. The check its jurisdiction has upon crime is extraordinary from the fact that the inquiries held by this Court are instituted in the immediate neighbourhood of the occurrence which calls forth the intervention of the law, and that the investigations are conducted by those well acquainted, as neighbours, or as residents in the locality, with the parties concerned, and with every circumstance in connexion with the case.

In the formation of the Coroner's Court what is found? A people's Court!—a Court in which justice is administered by the people, guided by the experience and advice of their own elected representative, the president of the Court being elected by the people. Here at once is provided a shield against oppression and injustice, should an arrogant, illiberal, and oppressive administration ever again vault into power. The public health is the most important feature in all State affairs: without this desideratum how can wealth and power be derived or maintained? Of health and life the Coroner's Court is peculiarly watchful, and its powers when properly carried out of chief importance; for while the Coroner's Court particularly attends to the physical condition of the community, bringing the deliberate murderer to justice, it at once pounces upon those cool and indifferent authorities or officials, who, although armed with the power of preventing the breaking out or the spread of dire disease, yet allow a whole population to be decimated through the existence of some crying evil, permitting their unfortunate and unsuspecting charge to wither away to the cold grave before their eyes, without adopting those steps which might check such a flagrant destruction of human life. Thomson, in his "Seasons," thus well describes a state of things arising from such unpardonable neglect and official apathy:—

> " When o'er this world by equinoctial rains
>   Flooded immense, looks out the joyless sun,
>   And draws the copious stream from swampy fens,
>   Where putrefaction into life ferments,
>   And breathes destructive myriads ; or from woods,
>   Impenetrable shades, recesses foul ;
>   In vapours rank and blue, corruption wrapt,

> Whose gloomy horrors yet no desperate foot
> Has ever dar'd to pierce ; then wasteful, forth
> Walks the dire power of pestilent disease,
> A thousand hideous fiends her course attend,
> Sick nature blasting, and, to heartless woe,
> And feeble desolation, casting down
> The towering hopes, and all the pride of man.
>   *   *   *   *   *
>   *   *   *   Her awful rage
> The brute escapes ; man is her destined prey."

In life's struggle pecuniary advancement is too eagerly looked for as the great consideration. Thousands make it their all absorbing thought, but how vain these pecuniary advantages, these mental calculations, these buoyant hopes without health ? *Non est vivere sed valere vita.* The Coroner's Court, keen and watchful under all circumstances, gives such confidence that the mind can pursue its bent stealthily, mature its hopes, and feel that a protection is thrown around the main-spring of its very existence.

This Court by its powerful agency pursues the deliberate murderer, awes those who would otherwise imbrue their hands in the blood of their fellow-creatures, commiserates the condition of the wretched poor and unfortunate, and tears with just, yet pitiless hands, the mask from the hypocritical or unfeeling official.

It is fearful to contemplate the abuses of the sanatory and physical condition of the people, and the social and moral results which would arise did not this Court exist.

Open murder and secret crime might run riot,

or from inattention to sanatory regulations, the population be so destroyed or physically weakened that the whole frame work of society would be broken up—the operative and commercial elements all but destroyed, or at least hurled into such a state of prostration, that our flourishing empire, the wonder of the world, would be brought to utter ruin—nay, the descendants of a warlike race become the puny sickly playthings of more stalwart arms, and their once free and boasted land scorned and despised among the nations.

Do not arguments like these prove that such an institution, democratic as it is from its peculiar and wise formation, is of necessity one of the most important this country possesses?

But what do we find in the present day? Another tribunal perfectly arbitrary, breathing throughout that system obnoxious to the English and trans-atlantic people, centralization springing up, and attempting to abrogate the authority of this people's Court. The new police system which it was found necessary to establish, or rather re-model, in order to check a minor scale of crime, and bring the petty offender to justice, takes upon itself not only seriously to interfere with, but actually to ridicule, the Coroner's administration. Ah! sad it will be for the people if such interference is allowed to continue; the end will be the complete annihilation of a Court, the last remnant of a recognition of the people untrammelled by Crown officers. Justice will be hoodwinked, human life become a matter of pounds, shillings, and pence. Laws thus placed entirely under an uncontrolled power against which there is no appeal, will afford to the people only a system of oppression under which they may become victims without either oppressors or murderers being brought to justice. This is particularly evident in the case of some popular disturbance; the people might have a just cause to raise their voice, but the controlling power would be found the stronger party. That this is no overdrawn statement one or two illustrations will confirm. Citizens were ruthlessly maltreated at Birmingham during the meetings held previous to the breaking out of the riots there. On that occasion the police came behind the people at an open air meeting and commenced felling them with their batons like cattle, and that too before any disturbance occurred. More recently in Hyde-park, unoffending men, women, and even children, were shamefully illused. Such again may be the conduct of an armed force in another popular agitation, and more painful to surmise, life may be sacrificed; but what justice can follow if, as it has been proposed, any investigation that may take place shall be entirely in the hands of the police. Does this savour of English ideas, or continental JUSTICE? Does it not rather exhibit a system of Neapolitan Sbirri tactics, than English law? Indeed, enough might be drawn from the disclosures made respecting the conduct of the police during the Hyde-park disturbances without, perhaps, having alluded to Birmingham,—*Ex pede Her-*

culem, it is unnecessary to point to other instances similarly exhibiting such a spirit of oppression and brutality. What, therefore, would be the result if uncontrolled power were given to such a body under a *régime* Neapolitan in its executive.

The public mind cannot be too seriously impressed with the consequences that would certainly arise, were they placed solely under the control of a power like that of the police in matters relating to life and death.

The present mischievous and uncalled for interference of stipendiary magistrates, and the police, with the Coroner's important duties, should be at once denounced by the public voice.

How dangerous will such an interference become if it goes on unchecked, and a tribunal be established against whose decisions there is no appeal.

The anomalous state of the law regarding the ability to appeal against a police magistrate's, or County Court judge's decision, has already attracted the special attention of several leading legal representatives. Amongst the foremost to dissent from such an arbitrary power is Lord Brougham.

It should, indeed, be well observed that *there is no appeal* against a police magistrate's summary decision, and yet it is urged to place the people more fully under this harsh and exceedingly repulsive *régime.*

In the event of the Coroner's Court being abolished, an example of the unjust working of such a system may be quoted as follows.

A citizen is alleged to have been killed by a

policeman for whose acts, according to the law of England, the master or employer, in the person of the magistrate or the police commissioners, is responsible; but an investigation being held before the very magistrate in whose district the crime is said to have been committed, he takes a view of the affair directly in favour of the accused, and decides accordingly by dismissing the charge.

There is *no appeal* from this decision; no further inquiry, and society may be thus outraged and the law placed at defiance by the veto of one man. The consequences resulting from such a system are really too frightful to contemplate.

The conflicting proceedings arising from time to time, owing to the animus exhibited by Metropolitan magistrates towards the Coroner's Court, proves that an entirely new system is required to place the two courts upon a better understanding with regard to each other, and through which one court will not interfere with the administration of justice in the other.

The office of the Coroner is of too important a character to be dealt with lightly. It embraces such special duties and considerations that it is essential that the power of the Court should, by remodelling the whole system, be clearly defined, and at the same time, by enlarging its powers, the Court should obtain that *status* which it deserves in the administration of justice.

Now, proceeding to analyse the duties of the Coroner, it will be found, unfortunately, that the office has degenerated and become in its administration considerably restricted in those districts where Coroners allow themselves to become trammelled by the interference of the county magistrates until the inquiries are simply confined to some special case of suicide, sudden death, or evident murder.

Surely the office was intended to reach further ends than these. True, they form its principal duties, but the investigations should have a wider range, and should not only include cases enveloped in mystery and suspicion, but *every case* where the cause of *death is unknown*.

By holding inquests in cases where no suspicion of foul play is entertained, secret murder would be greatly, if not entirely prevented, for the simple reason that parties concerned would be ignorant as to whether an inquiry would take place or not, and be alarmed by the probability that an investigation *would* really be instituted.

Had such a system been in operation at Rugeley, how many dreadful murders and social crimes might have been prevented.

It is to be exceedingly regretted that in many counties, such as in Staffordshire, the office of Coroner is so restricted, through the interference of the county magistrates, that it has become almost useless.* Very few inquests take place, and, even when they are held, no *post mortem* examination is performed in the majority of cases. Now,

* It was stated before a Committee of the House of Commons in 1851, that the constabulary of Staffordshire were instructed not to furnish notices of deaths to the Coroners, except when crime was *suspected*. And the Coroners were informed

certainly, without the assistance of a *post mortem* examination in cases of sudden death, or in cases of death from supposed drowning, hanging, and the like, such investigations are perfectly useless. Had a few inquests been held at Rugeley in cases of natural death, Palmer, coward as his atrocious system of murder proved him to be, would never have had the hardihood to carry out his poisonings, because he would have had before his eyes *the possibility* of an investigation taking place on his first victim. Surely it is better and more humane to prevent than to punish crime, and one inquiry at the period this wretched man premeditated his awful deeds might have appalled, and his murderous intentions at once failed him.

The duties of the Coroner require to be enlarged, and they should be permitted to be carried out with greater freedom, dignity, and respect.

In the first place, by all means let the Coroner be as heretofore, in those districts where such a proceeding as in the county of Middlesex has always been adopted, elected by the people, rather extending than restricting this representative system. This could be done by the election taking place at the hands of the Parliamentary voters, instead of leaving it, as at present, with the freeholders and landed proprietors.

The Coroner should have his authority recognised as that of a magistrate appointed by the Crown, and

that if they held inquests in such cases, their fees would be disallowed. Under these regulations Palmer committed several murders.—Extract from letter of Dr. Farr, Registrar-General. Also see article in the Appendix, p. 63.

he should most certainly have a seat on the County Bench.

The office should not be degraded by in one point of view the duties being paid for *by the work done.* It is degraded when the Coroner is liable to be charged as an extortioner, which in plain terms is simply the case when the county magistrates take upon themselves to condemn as unnecessary a number of inquiries, and disallow the fees charged by him.

To prevent this, the Coroner should be paid an annual salary, which could be revised every three years, and decreased if on the triennial average the duties were found to be lighter than before. This would be more respectable for the true administration of justice, and, in fact, more economical to the State.

If a Metropolitan Coroner, his salary could be fixed according to that of the Metropolitan stipendiary magistrates, or according to the extent of the district he had charge over. The latter course would be more desirable in the appointment of Provincial Coroners.

The question may arise, who shall fix the salary of the Coroners? This is a highly important, although an after consideration, should these suggestions be carried out. Should it meet with the concurrence of the majority of the electors, the question of salary might be left with the Crown at the outset, and a triennial revision allowed to be retained by the County Bench, subject to an appeal if the revision were not considered a just and equitable one.

Certain fixed Courts should be appointed where Coroner's inquiries could be held. Expensive new buildings for that purpose would be unnecessary, as an office adjoining the district police court could be set apart, or the investigations could be held in the vestry hall, or other parochial offices, such as in the board rooms of workhouses, &c. In such districts as in Middlesex, Westminster, and the City of London, it would require several suitable buildings in various localities to meet the requirements of the population. This accommodation could be easily had in the parochial offices and at police courts. In the case of police courts, it invariably happens there are two courts, one being generally unoccupied, and a magistrate's room on other occasions could give the necessary accommodation. In parochial offices, besides a board room, there are invariably a number of commodious committee and waiting rooms set apart for the ratepayers, which are generally vacant four or five days out of the week.

There is no wish in these suggestions to interfere with the small fee at present allowed to licensed victuallers for the accommodation afforded to the Coroner, but the whole object aimed at is that of effecting a great public service, and, in a pecuniary point of view of lessening the county rates, which now fall so heavily on not only the Licensed Victuallers' body, but every class of trade. The temporary gain to the Licensed Victuallers for giving accommodation is small, but by the adoption of the system alluded to in the foregoing paragraph the gain in a more extended sense would be large, for be it observed, that in every fee the charge on the county rate is double, and it is highly probable that for 3*s*. 6*d*. the licensed victualler receives for the use of a room to hold a Coroner's inquiry in, he has to pay double and sometimes treble that sum back to the county. At all events, it is very certain that the tendering of a fee to the licensed victualler or a ratepayer as a juror under such circumstances is a perfect farce, as the same is exacted at a future period from those parties on the county rates. The licensed victualler, in fact, gets no payment for the accommodation he affords and the great inconvenience he is too often put to, as well as expense, for lighting, fire, &c.

The next important consideration in the formation of the Court is the appointment of juries, a matter which specially requires revision, and an almost entire change.

With all such juries the burden principally falls upon the trader and working man. The professional class and those of independent means invariably escape; at least, it is pretty certain that in nineteen Coroner's Juries out of twenty the jury is composed of tradesmen and persons who are put to extreme inconvenience by so attending.

Now this is unjust, and arises from the indiscriminate manner in which such juries are summoned; the borough lists not being taken in many districts, as in the Superior Courts and at the Sessions, for a clue to those who are bound to attend as jurors, and whose names should be taken in rotation.

To effect a change in the present Coroner's Jury system, let the jury be composed of thirteen *inhabitant householders*—six professional men and seven tradesmen.

It frequently happens twenty persons are unnecessarily summoned on a Coroner's Jury in order to obtain a proper number, viz. twelve or thirteen together. This is a very loose way of proceeding, and gives needless trouble both to the summoning officers and those parties who attend as a majority, and are consequently not required to be sworn.

It has also often happened that perfect strangers, mere passers-by, have been stopped and empanneled on a Coroner's Jury in order to form the proper number,—evidently a very improper proceeding, as a passer-by might really be a friend or partizan of an accused person, even the unknown murderer, who would thus throw himself in the way to be summoned, and by the influence he might bring to bear, through a superior judgment, upon his fellow jurors, imperil the fair administration of justice.

Such an event it will be acknowledged is probable, seeing, as a close observer of legal matters can, that it often happens the minds of a whole jury are led and biassed by a single juryman.*

* "On reaching the room (upon retiring), there was a dead silence for about twenty minutes. A discussion of the facts that had been laid before us was then commenced, and it lasted for about ten minutes, after which each man took pen and paper and wrote his decision and name, it having been agreed that no one should pronounce his opinion, lest any other should *receive a bias.*"—Letter from a Juror on the trial of Palmer.

All this could be prevented by a stricter rule being observed in the summoning of such Juries. Let them be subpœnaed as at Sessions; and, if not punctual in attendance, the usual fine should be at once imposed. This proceeding would lead to a regular attendance on the part of those summoned, and there would be no occasion to call together more than the required number to form the Jury; and, in the end, this proceeding would gain more respect and consideration for the Court.

As to the formation of the Jury by the empanneling of six professional men and seven tradesmen or men in business. Again remarking that it does not appear just that tradesmen should be solely enforced to perform such onerous duties, when it is considered that they have also to serve on all other Juries, besides being called upon to administer local affairs, it should be noted that a Coroner's inquiry, involving as it does a final decision in the generality of cases, is a most important subject for searching investigation. There are not two juries, a Grand Jury and a Petty Jury, concerned, but simply one; and on the judgment of this one body a deliberate decision depends, which, if the result should criminate any person or persons, cannot be set aside by a Grand Jury or any such power which rules other panels in the superior Criminal Courts, but the case must be brought to trial. Therefore the same parties liable to be summoned to the Old Bailey and other Courts should bear an equal burden of the duties imposed by investigations in the Coroner's; and by this the character of the Court would be raised, and many important questions of a scientific character, through the admixture of professional knowledge, could be properly solved and decided.

It is frequently the case that Coroner's juries are summoned an hour (and even less time is allowed), before an inquiry takes place. The result is that, under such circumstances, juries often go to investigations in bad spirit; they are more absorbed in general business matters of life than the administration of justice; and the consequence is, that many most important inquiries, which demanded long and patient consideration, are hurried over, to the great discredit of the Court. To prevent this, some hours, say twelve at the least, should intervene, unless the sultriness of the season calls for a speedier investigation, owing to decomposition more rapidly setting in than in cold weather, between the summoning of the jury and the holding the inquiry. Where jurors could not attend through illness, they should at once inform the summoning officer, who then upon the production of a medical certificate, or such like sufficient reason for non-attendance, on the ground of domestic affliction, and similar causes, should find a substitute by summoning that person whose name stood next on the list of voters.

The jury should be summoned to meet at the house or late residence of the deceased; and there, having been sworn, and seen that the body was properly identified—for in some cases identification has been incomplete, through the want of such a practice—they should proceed with the Coroner to the nearest Court, and enter upon the evidence, if an adjournment *in limine* upon viewing the remains was not agreed upon.

All fines should be strictly enforced, as in other Courts, unless good and sufficient grounds could be shown by the absentee for his contempt of Court in not appearing to the summons.

The picking juries out of the regular jury lists would give great satisfaction, as it does where the system is pursued in many districts of Westminster, for a juror may not thus have to attend more than once in six or twelve months; while at present, through such juries being indiscriminately summoned from the immediate neighbourhood of the death, a tradesman is often called out two and three times a-week to attend Coroners' investigations. The injustice of this part of the present system is plainly observable in the vicinity of workhouses and hospitals, which institutions give a wide scope to the duties of the Coroner, and where the residents of the locality are being continually summoned upon Coroners' juries.

The particular duties and powers of the Coroner's Court now come under review, and this part of the question demands most serious and impartial consideration.

Primarily the duties ought to be as to causes of death, and the cases in which such inquiries are held should be indispensably as follows:—

1. In all cases of sudden death; that is, where the person falls lifeless, is found dead, dies

without medical attendance, or under such circumstances by a sudden seizure as to leave his death unaccountable, so that the medical attendant called in at the time cannot certify *the exact cause* without performing an internal examination of the body, or, as such a proceeding is now technically termed, a *post-mortem.*

In all cases like these, there should be such an examination, and an analysis made of the contents of the stomach, intestines, and other portions of the body. An analysis is rendered necessary; for there is no reason in presuming that because the heart, lungs, brain, kidneys, liver, or other prominent organs, may be diseased, that the person has necessarily died of such disease. The deceased may have suffered from the disease, perhaps, for years previously, and no human reason could in all probability be shown for life not being continued. The deceased might therefore have died from poison. The latter presumption stands as good as the one that he died from disease. The medical witness who performed the *post-mortem* examination would state he found certain appearances of disease which were of long standing, and which were sufficient to account for death; but he could not at the same time swear, without an analytical examination, that there was no poison in the system, which when the circumstances of the case were more rigidly pursued might be found to have had some connexion with the death. An analytical examination would at once settle all doubts. It should be strictly enforced that a careful analysis should be made, and the result, with the appearances of disease discovered, laid before the Court by the medical witness.

At present, in the Coroner's warrant, authorising the making a *post-mortem* examination, it is stated that, *if necessary*, an analysis shall be made; but in very few cases is any performed, the anatomist being satisfied by the discovery of disease in some vital organ; and it might be remarked, that there are very few medical men competent to perform a proper analysis. When such an examination is required, it is generally by some professor who has devoted his whole time to analytical researches; and therefore it will be necessary, in another part of this treatise, to allude to the subject again. Here it is intended to impress upon the reader the great necessity for the orders of the Coroner to be more imperative. Let not the Coroner leave it to the whim of a medical man to perform an analysis by inserting in his warrant, *if necessary*, but the words, *an analysis shall also be made.*

2. Inquests should be held in all cases of deaths from violence, or alleged violence.

Now in such inquiries, if it should be proved that direct suspicion existed against any party or parties respecting the death of the deceased, it ought to be in the power of the Coroner to issue a warrant for the apprehension of such party or parties, and order a remand, if necessary, the Houses of Detention and jails being placed at the disposal of the Coroner for such purposes as at present they are to the magistrates. There can be no doubt but that the power of arrest and remand, as also of bailing, should be placed in the hands of the Coroner without delay, as it is not proper an accused person should be at large while a Coroner's inquiry is pending—the charge being one, perhaps, of murder—or that an innocent person should be detained in durance vile while an accusation is being investigated. At present the Coroner can only order arrest and detention upon the verdict of the jury criminating any party or parties, as is evident from the wording of his warrants.

No. 1. Warrant of Apprehension.

" To all constables, headboroughs, &c.—

" To wit. Whereas by an inquisition taken before me, one of Her Majesty's Coroners for the said county of   , this   day of   , at the parish of   , in the said county of   , on view of the body of A. A., then lying dead, one   late of the parish of   , in the said county, stands charged with the wilful murder of the said A. A. These are, therefore, by virtue of my office, in Her Majesty's name, to charge and command you and every of you, that you or some or one of you without delay do apprehend, &c."

No. 2. Warrant of Detainer.

" To the keeper of Her Majesty's jail of   ,—

" To wit. Whereas you have in your custody the body of   , and whereas by an inquisition taken before me, one of Her Majesty's Coroners for the said county of   , the day and year hereunder written, at the parish of   in the said county on view of the body of A. A. then and there lying dead, he the said   stands charged with the wilful murder of the said A. A. These are, therefore, in Her

Majesty's name, by virtue of my office, to charge and command you to detain and keep in your custody the body of the said   until he shall be thence discharged by due course of law, and for your so doing this is your warrant, &c."

The Coroner, in cases where casualties arose from *culpable neglect*, not amounting to *criminal careless-ness*, should have the power upon the decision of the jury to that effect, to fine the party or parties guilty of such negligence, the fine not to amount to more than 100*l.*, and not be less than 5*s.* In default of payment committal should follow, after proper notice had been given fixing the payment of the fine within a certain period. If this system of fining were adopted in the Coroner's Court, it would assuredly be the means of saving many lives, for there is nothing so much affects the generality of people as pecuniary liability. Observe the present awful annual sacrifice of life in the Metropolis amongst children through the carelessness of parents and nurses leaving them alone with fire and other dangerous appliances.

The system of fining would meet another great evil which might be reasonably alluded to here—the careless dispensing of medicines, and the indiscriminate sale of poisonous drugs and compounds. Where it was proved that a dispenser of medicines, or any individual practising the same business, be he qualified or not, had carelessly supplied dangerous medicines, or without restriction sold poisons to whoever applied for them, either for *suicidal purposes*, or otherwise, let a severe fine be imposed if the act did not amount to one of a criminal character, such as in a case of murder. In France fine and imprisonment are often imposed for such offences, and this in many cases would no doubt be advisable in this country. The offence might be of so grave a character that the accused could be fined, and, at the same time, committed to take his trial on a *criminal charge*. This would soon put an end to careless dispensing; and "medical quacks," those individuals who, without qualification or knowledge, prey upon the vitals of human life, and send thousands annually to their graves, either by adopting a system of treatment quite contrary to what should be pursued for the cure of disease, or else by their "do-nothing" system, could by this proceeding be fairly dealt with as on the Continent.

Apothecaries and chymists, so far as the sale of poisons and bad medicines are concerned, could be placed under the immediate control of the Coroner's Court, with power being granted to the latter to license all such qualified traders. No poisons should be sold unless for medicinal purposes, and it should be strictly laid down that all poisonous mixtures or ingredients sent out should bear a significant and special mark upon them. All poisonous drugs or embrocations should be dispensed in peculiarly shaped bottles formed of coloured glass—red being the most conspicuous—as well as being labelled "Poison," and poisonous ingredients in a dry state should be sent out in coloured paper—say red also—with the word "Poison" emblazoned on the package or powder. The Coroner should be empowered as the Apothecaries' Company are within the City of London to enter all apothecaries' and chymists' shops, and examine as to whether proper precautions were taken in the dispensing of poisonous drugs and compounds. All poisons should be kept apart from other medicines, in conspicuously shaped and coloured bottles. If strict rules like these had been enforced years ago, how many lamentable occurrences arising from the careless dispensing and disposal of poisonous medicines might have been averted. It would be as well for the Coroner in his examination to have a properly qualified medical man or analytical chymist with him, as also a jury; and upon the decision of the latter a fine might be imposed. If the offence should be continued, imprisonment and fine ought to follow; and for a third offence, considering all such persons were duly qualified, the license should be entirely withdrawn, and the offender debarred from in future following that profession, as human life is not to be so wantonly sacrificed.

3. Coroners' inquiries should certainly be held in cases of suspected arson, or where a conflagration was at all enshrouded in mystery and suspicion, for the lives of Her Majesty's subjects are thereby endangered. It should be the duty of the Coroner to hold an investigation in all such cases, and the proceedings should be looked upon with serious importance, for although life might not have been sacrificed, yet it has been exposed to danger, and placed in extreme jeopardy. It should also be competent for the Coroner

in such inquiries, after consulting with the jury, to order the arrest and detention of any party or parties who might be implicated, or upon whom suspicion rested, until the jury had arrived at a final decision.

4. As sanatory matters involve questions of superlative importance respecting the health of the community at large, it should be competent for the Coroner to call together a Jury and investigate any existing sanatory evils, and upon the decision of the Jury order, under certain penalties, the abatement of such evils, as also the effecting the improvements deemed necessary. These improvements might be (according to the responsibility), ordered to be carried out, either at the expense of the owner or owners of the property where the evils existed, or by enforcing the local authorities to carry out those alterations. Indeed the latter course, considering the present sanatory staff connected with local representation through the new Metropolis Local Management Act, might be considered the most advisable. The district authorities could be authorized to have the improvements recommended, strictly carried out, and, if necessary, effect such improvements themselves at the cost of the proprietor or proprietors. This, in a great measure, would prevent an interference with local authority, and at the same time meet every public requirement.

The Medical Officer of Health for the district should, when any such inquiry took place, be summoned, and his special attention could be directed to the future sanatory welfare of the neighbourhood.

If after these proceedings the evils continued unabated, the Coroner should be empowered by the decision of the jury who previously investigated the matter, to indict, on the evidence then taken, the culpable parties at the sessions. A more serious view of the case should be conceived if any mortality arose from diseases engendered by the still filthy state of the locality. An inquiry into such mortality being forthwith held by the Coroner and another jury, and the culpable party or parties, be they Government Commissioners, local authorities, medical officers of health, or private individuals—the owners of the property—should be deemed responsible for any loss of life originating from their neglect. Their responsibility would be very serious if they had pertinaciously refused to carry out the improvements previously ordered, so as to avert such a calamity as a sacrifice of human life. Indeed, they would be deemed as responsible and culpable as though death had been occasioned by manual violence, and they might be charged according to the weight of their offence either under the head of *wilful murder* or *manslaughter*.

To show the nice line drawn between these two crimes a quotation from a work on the subject by Sir John Jervis, will be found instructive :—

"Manslaughter is the unlawful killing of another without malice, either express or implied; and is either voluntary, from sudden transport of passion, or involuntary, arising from the commission of some unlawful act, or from the pursuit of some lawful act, criminally or improperly performed. The absence of malice is, as has been already observed, the main distinction between this species of homicide and murder, and though manslaughter is in its degree felonious, and in the eyes of the law criminal, yet it is imputed by the benignity of the law to the infirmity of human nature."

Again he observes:—

" Correction by privation and ill-treatment will, if death ensue, be sufficient to constitute this offence; for *active and personal violence* is not necessary."

It is to be regretted that under existing circumstances too many officials who are really morally guilty, escape the just legal punishment due to their offences. The guilt consists in their neglecting the imperative duties imposed on them by law, and which they accept of their own free will and accord. By thus punishing the agents of so iniquitous a system, it would immediately give to it a check, and by placing such a power in the hands of the Coroner's Court, a strict watch would be kept on all officials engaged in carrying out the sanatory and other laws connected with the health, welfare, and life of the public, and they would be taught not only the strict rules of justice, but also those of humanity.

Under the Metropolis Local Management Act a large staff of sanatory officers were appointed in the various parishes throughout London. There ought surely to be some greater and more impartial supervision of this important body than that afforded by the local authorities, and this would be met with in the Coroner. What court is more competent to judge of the conduct of such sanatory officers than the Coroner's? This Court deals with all matters concerning life and death, and the greatest responsibility should be vested in it over all sanatory matters. In fact it is very clear that this new staff of sanatory officers will become in many instances a non-effective body, unless some impartial control is secured whereby they can be enforced to perform their duty, and held criminally responsible for neglecting it. It will not do in the present day to leave the public health in the hands of irresponsible agents.

The duties of the Medical Officers of Health, under the new Act, are, according to Sec. cxxxii. of that enactment, as follows :—

"Every Vestry and District Board shall, from time to time, appoint one or more legally qualified medical practitioner or practitioners, of skill and experience, to inspect and report periodically upon the sanatory condition of their parish or district, to ascertain the existence of disease, more especially epidemics increasing the rate of mortality, and to point out the existence of any nuisance or other local causes which are likely to originate and maintain such disease and injuriously affect the health of the inhabitants, and to take cognizance of the fact of the existence of any contagious or epidemic diseases, and to point out the most efficacious mode of checking or preventing the spread of such diseases. And also to point out the most efficient modes for the ventilation of churches, chapels, schools, lodging houses, and other public edifices within the parish or district, and to perform any other duties of a like nature which may be required of him or them, and such persons shall be called 'Medical Officers of Health,' and it shall be lawful for the Vestry or Board to pay to every such officer such salary as they may think fit, and also to remove any such officer at the pleasure of such Vestry or Board."

The Act then goes on to appoint other sanatory officers, in the shape of Inspectors of Nuisances, and the greatest consideration is observed for protecting the public health, but still there is wanted that impartial check upon this department which can alone be obtained by the whole staff being placed, to a certain extent, under the supervision of the Coroner's Court.

The law is very imperative, but from the want of a proper supervision in how many instances does it remain a dead letter?

It does not require comment on any particular locality of the Metropolis to show that sanatory regulations require to be more strictly enforced. Go to the four quarters of the Metropolis and walk through its filthy lanes, its confined courts, and baneful districts fearfully impregnated with an atmosphere of disease and death. There is evidence of neglect in every direction, which only a sweeping supervision such as that recommended can remove. This great and increasing city requires such an executive Government as will at once place it in a wholesome and proper sanatory condition.

How apt is one when considering this subject and reviewing objections that may be raised, to warmly exclaim,

" Salus Populi suprema lex."

5. The same law for strictly supervising the duties of Sanatory Officers could be enforced as well on parochial authorities and officials concerned in the distribution of parish relief, and indeed all

other bodies entrusted with the charge of human life. They should as certainly be punished when it is proved that through their indifference, neglect, or harshness, any loss of life has taken place. It would be useless and painful to instance cases demanding such interference. The newspapers for years past have been filled with the recital of tales of misery and cruelty in which death has resulted from the callous indifference, neglect, and harshness of parochial officials, and the public been sufficiently pained by such heartrending stories without citing them anew.

The parties concerned in such shocking scenes were according to the present state of the law not *legally guilty*, notwithstanding the high *moral responsibility* they had incurred.

An alteration of this anomalous state of things as here recommended, would make the parochial official, who refused that relief which the law directs *shall* be awarded to the poor and destitute, criminally responsible for any death that arose in consequence, either from suicide, or the want of the common necessaries of life. Let not such cruel indifference go unpunished. Let not so ridiculous a bar be drawn across moral guilt and its proper punishment.

Indeed in some special cases recorded by Sir John Jervis, there will be found those in which this neglect is proved to amount to " wilful murder," and it is to be regretted that the law is not now as vigorously carried out, instead of being trammelled with absurd addenda censuring certain parties for high moral guilt.

In one case thus recorded, the indictment charged an accused with "*wilful murder*," as

"In the county aforesaid, feloniously, wilfully, and of malice aforethought, did neglect, omit, and refuse to give, and administer, and to permit, and suffer to be given, and administered to him, the said R——, sufficient meat and drink necessary for the support and maintenance of the body of him, the said R——, &c."

And in the second case the party was charged with the capital offence, *through causing death by forcing the deceased into the street while sick.*

Leaving this part of the subject, the next that comes under consideration is with respect to the verdicts of Coroners' Juries, which likewise require great amendment on the present system.

Their verdicts are at present so confined that Coroners' Juries have frequently to travel out of their legitimate rules, and pass censures upon parties concerned, or they animadvert upon a particular system requiring in their opinion amendment, or entire repeal. This is certainly an abuse which has crept into the office, for Juries have no more right to adopt such a course than any unauthorised or illegal assembly.

It might be appropriate to note on this subject that in giving judgment in a case tried in the Court of Queen's Bench, on May 8th, 1844, [The Queen *v.* the Coroner of the City of London,] Lord Chief Justice Denman said, that the part of the finding, which properly constituted the verdict, was that which stated the cause and manner of death, and the state of the deceased at the time. All the rest was upon matter altogether irrelevant. The jury had no right to go out of their way for the purpose of expressing their opinion upon a matter which was not in issue before them, and it was not at all certain, that in so doing in the present case, they had not rendered themselves liable to the usual consequences of the publication of a libel.

Sir John Jervis under the head of "Verdict" in his work on the "Office and Duties of Coroners," already quoted, says, with respect to the decision of Coroners' Juries:

"The verdict or finding of the Coroners' Jury is equivalent to an indictment, and must be stated with the same legal certainty and precision; it must not be repugnant nor inconsistent; and the charge must be direct and positive."

The verdict should be "Aye" or "Nay," but it would at the same time be very useful for the Scotch verdict "Not Proven" to be introduced into the Coroner's Court where a final decision is in the hands of the Jury.

The cases brought before the Coroner's Court are often of an exceedingly conflicting character, and it is impossible in many instances to say what is the precise cause of death. While there may be a great suspicion against any party or parties, yet there is not sufficient legal proof to indict on a criminal charge, and, therefore, it would be useless to put the county to an unnecessary expense by such a prosecution. The police magistrates simply appear as prosecutors, and, therefore, only evidence against the accused is taken before a committal for trial. The result is, that many cases so disposed of are dismissed at the superior court, and the county is saddled with the unnecessary expense incurred by the prosecution. The Coroner's Jury hear both sides of the case, the accusation and the defence, and decide at once upon both, thereby greatly decreasing the county expenditure by preventing unsupported prosecutions. In cases thus alluded to, the system of fining would be very apropos. It would do away with the illegal addenda system, and prove more severe on the party or parties implicated.

The medical evidence upon which, in a great measure, all such inquiries depend, is often very unsatisfactory. Therefore, in cases where a party has been arrested on great suspicion, and the medical and other evidence is inconclusive, but the suspicion still remains, a verdict of " *Not Proven* " might reasonably be introduced. The suspected party could then be discharged ; but, at any future period, if the case be one of suspected " *Wilful Murder* " or " *Manslaughter*," it should be in the power of the Lord Chief Justice, upon more conclusive evidence arising, to order a further investigation to take place.

After a verdict of " *Not Proven* " had been returned, it would be a desirable course to issue a *non exeat e regno*, restraining the suspected party from leaving the country within a certain period, as evidence of a conclusive nature might in the meantime transpire. Upon the expiration of the *non exeat*, the party could be considered discharged from further restraint; but, as at present, in charges of homicide, the accused should be liable to be again arrested if evidence was forthcoming proving the crime.

The next important matter for consideration is as to the officers attached to the Coroner's Court, and their duties.

In the first place, a thorough reorganization of this department is called for, and an increase of the staff will be rendered essentially necessary for the due and impartial administration of justice. This increase will be found not only just but economical.

The Coroner ought to have a deputy, at least in those districts, such as in the county of Middlesex, and the city of London, where the area is very extensive, and the population numerous. This deputy might be appointed by the Coroner, under the sanction of the Secretary of State for the Home Department, at a set salary, adequate to the duties imposed.

It should be necessary for the deputy-Coroner, if not a medical man, to be well versed in medical jurisprudence, and thoroughly acquainted with the duties of the office.

Next in importance—and this will be an increase of the staff necessary for the proper fulfilment of the duties of the Coroner—is the appointment of a public prosecutor. He should be a member of the legal profession well versed in medical jurisprudence, and attend inquiries in all cases

of alleged murder, arson, defective sanatory regulations, &c. It would be his duty to lay the
facts of the case before the Court on the side of
the prosecution, and call the necessary witnesses,
the public prosecutor to be bound over to prosecute, should the case be sent for trial before
another tribunal.

The importance and necessity for appointing an
officer like this in every Court of Justice is very
evident ; and it is only following in the opinions of
such legal advisers as Lord Brougham, by alluding
to such an appointment.

The public prosecutor is more especially required
where human life is the object of investigation ;
and it is very painful to observe that, under existing
rules, many foul murders go unpunished through
the want of such an officer.

A short time back, an abominable murder was
committed at St. Alban's. Certain implicated
parties were arrested, and committed to take their
trial for the offence at the assizes. No prosecutor,
however, appeared, when the gaol delivery took
place, and the Judge before whom the case came
considered it so heinous a crime, that, instead of
discharging the accused, he remanded them to
the next assize, in order to give an opportunity
for the prosecution to be proceeded with. Thus
they were remanded several assizes, and at length
they were discharged, as no prosecutor appeared.

In permitting such an officer to act, due regard
should be had to the interest of the party or

parties implicated, by allowing legal representatives to attend on their behalf and proceed with a defence, for by such a course much trouble and expence would be prevented, as no necessity might arise, on hearing both sides, to send the case for trial.

The public prosecutor would be the poor man's representative in all cases of alleged parochial inhumanity and neglect, as also where the sanatory condition of the dwellings of the working-classes, and the poorer population, was the subject for inquiry.

At present, while the parochial authorities and other powerful bodies are represented, the poor man stands alone, and the consequence is that he is often beaten out of Court by the shrewdness and tact of the parties he thought proper as a matter of justice to complain of. Indeed, such an officer should be appointed by the Government to act as the poor man's representative at the administration of parochial relief.

Another object tending to the welfare and inestimable benefit of the public health would be gained by the appointment of this officer in the Coroner's Court. It has been a vexed question how to deal with a nefarious class of traders—those who adulterate and poison the common necessaries of life. The question has been fully discussed in Parliament, and a Committee of the House of Commons gleaned sufficient upon which to form a special Bill to meet so great and injurious a grievance, but there seems to be a difficulty as to the manner in which the evil shall be eradicated. This could be at once solved, and the evil without further delay removed by vesting such power in the Coroner's Court as would enable the public prosecutor to proceed against adulterators, and insist on fine and imprisonment, as in the case of delinquent apothecaries, and all such traders reckless of health and life.

With the institution of public prosecutor it would be of importance to consider the desirability of appointing a public sanatory officer. He should be a medical man of eminence, whose opinion could be called in upon all medical, sanatory, and analytical points. This officer would prove highly useful in cases where a prosecution took place against persons who flagrantly injured the public health by adulterating the commodities of life, and those who scandalously allowed disease and death to become rampant through the neglect of sanatory regulations.

The duties of summoning officer could be left as at present in the hands of the parish constables, with, perhaps, a slight revision of their duties.

Immediately upon receiving notice of a case apparently demanding an inquiry, the constable ought to enter the whole circumstances in a legible form in a book kept for that purpose, and forward a copy of the same to the Coroner. The Coroner, having reviewed the whole facts of the case, and having entered the same in an office journal, should decide whether an inquiry was necessary or not.

Let it be well understood that in all cases

of death from alleged violence, or even supposed natural causes, an inquiry should be held where there was no medical certificate, and no medical man should be permitted, under pain of penalty,—the consequences resulting from such a proceeding being looked upon as a contempt of Court,—to give a certificate who had not seen the deceased before death.

Such a rule as this is very necessary, and it should be most strictly enforced, for at present medical men frequently give certificates as to the cause of death when they have only been called in at the period of demise, or immediately after, and they really can know nothing whatever of the precise cause.

To show to what a frightful extent this dangerous system prevails, in one case which took place some years ago, a medical man gave a certificate that a person of property, who had been living under such circumstances that his family wished to conceal the real facts, had died a natural death. Rumours got afloat that all was not right, and a Coroner's inquest was ordered to be held. When the Coroner and Jury went to view the deceased's remains there was nothing particular in the appearance of the body to attract the attention of an ordinary observer, although in all probability there were those exsanguineous appearances as proved something wrong to the experienced eye of the Coroner (Mr. Wakley). The corpse had been decently laid out, and a cravat enveloped the neck. The Coroner ordered the cravat to be removed, when behold a gaping wound presented itself in the throat: *the deceased had committed suicide, and not died a natural death.* Fortunately for the parties concerned—considering what circumstantial evidence will often lead to—it was clearly proved that he died by his own hands, but if such had not been the case this reckless mode of granting medical certificates might have led to the suspicion of a heinous crime having been committed, and the execution of an innocent person.

Some very rigorous rules should be resorted to without delay in order to deter unscrupulous members of the medical profession from acting in so disgraceful a manner. While preventing medical men from giving certificates under such circumstances, it should be strictly enforced that no *post mortem* examination should take place until the facts of the case had been laid before the Coroner, and he had issued his order for such an examination.

This part of the subject inadvertently brings one to comment upon the conduct of undertakers, who should be subject to severe penalties where they interred bodies without first obtaining the Registrar's or Coroner's certificate as to the precise cause of death, and no body should be interred without such certificate being shown to the officiating clergyman, or person in authority at the place of sepulture.

As a restriction on registrars no certificate of the cause of death should be received unless from the Coroner or a *duly qualified medical man,* who ought to state that he saw the deceased before death, how long he had attended the party, and the *precise* cause of death.

By this proceeding the present anomalous and ridiculous registration system, which is no protection whatever to life, would be completely remodelled and made a useful and important office.

Fine and imprisonment on undertakers failing to carry out the regulations of the Court should be imposed, the fine or imprisonment depending upon the serious character of the offence committed. Registrars would likewise be liable, under similar circumstances, to fine, imprisonment, and dismissal from office.

Such are a few propositions, which if adopted, can in the main be greatly improved upon, and more properly defined by an Act of Parliament.

A Bill for this purpose would not only effect a complete remodelling of this important office, but it would meet the requirements aimed at in Parliament by two other Acts, (which would therefore be unnecessary,) in a Bill for preventing adulterations, and a Bill for preventing medical quackery and the sale of poisons, as both these weighty subjects could be easily met and dealt with by the Coroner's Court under the new *régime*.

The subject is one demanding weighty consideration. That some Legislative interference is required in effecting a change in the present duties of the Court no one will for a moment deny, a slight change in the administration of its affairs, with the addition of such other duties as those pointed out, will make it one of the most popular and important institutions of the country.

Certainly it is necessary to lay down special rules for preventing magistrates and the police from *at all* interfering with the duties of the Coroner.

In all cases of death demanding a legal inquiry, and in all investigations relating to the public health, or in which human life is directly concerned, let the inquiries be confined to the Coroner's Court, and its jurisdiction should be alone disturbed by the head Coroner, the Lord Chief Justice, who upon reasonable and sufficient proof that justice had not been done could order the Government public prosecutor (supposing such an officer is appointed, and the system of public prosecutors be generally adopted), or, under present circumstances, the Attorney-General, to proceed further with the case before a superior Court. If on the trial it be proved that the Coroner had not properly fulfilled his duties, then it should be in the power of the Lord Chief Justice to remove him from his office and issue a writ for a new election. Moreover, if it were proved that the Coroner acted with a corrupt intention, he should be as open to a criminal prosecution as a magistrate.

Such a ruling power as this being vested in the hands of the Lord Chief Justice, is always necessary over an executive body.

So far as relates to Scotland it is a matter of serious consideration, whether it would not be highly desirable to have the same Coroner's Court and representative system carried out there as in other parts of the United Kingdom, as also the suggestions referring to registration, and thereby assimilate in such important matters the laws of the three countries, England, Scotland, and Ireland. In all three the stream of justice runs broad and deep, and, if occasionally it requires to be cleared from those weeds which interrupt its current, the act produces but a mere ripple of its wave, while,

" Labitur et labetur in omne volubilis ævum."

APPENDIX.

In the Paper presented by the Author to the Law Amendment Society, which with the proposed new measure, of which a sketch is here annexed, are now under consideration of a Special Committee of that body, occur the following passages :—

There is the law relating to infanticide—an exceedingly faulty and mischievous law, as it at present stands, and sad is it to contemplate the fearful annual sacrifice of infant life in this country by wilful acts of direct violence and neglect. Infanticide is a crime most difficult to prove. Therefore would it not be better to punish more rigorously for that which can be easily proved—viz., concealment of birth. The law for prosecuting in cases of concealment of birth is at present exceedingly abstruse, and indeed, according to the ruling of the judges, unintelligible. A charge of infanticide quickly breaks down if on no other evidence but that of the medical man, for what medical man can swear unless he was present at the time of the confinement whether the child was fully born or not when death ensued ? Then follows a charge of concealment of birth, and in the generality of cases this proves likewise a failure, for the judges will rule that unless it can be proved the body was placed in its intended final resting-place, the charge cannot be substantiated. This is surely making the law prosecute for concealment of death and not concealment of birth. To meet the evident requirements of the law on this subject, and as a preventive of the fearful crime of infanticide, it is very desirable to prosecute for concealment of birth, when it can be proved the mother concealed her pregnant state up to a certain period preceding confinement, or allowed herself to be confined without informing her friends or any person of her condition, so that medical aid and other assistance might be at hand at the time. Consider how many thousands of children perish for the want of proper assistance at the birth ! It is utterly impossible in such cases to prove one of deliberate and wilful murder, high as the crime may appear in a moral point of view, and under the existing system the wicked parent goes unpunished by human laws. Adopt searching prosecutions for concealment of birth, and this crying evil, "this murder most foul," will, if not entirely obliterated, yet be greatly checked. In Scotland the law is very rigorous in this respect; and why not, when the lives of thousands are at stake—thousands who may be saved to minister to the State, and be a stay and support of the constitution. Concealment of birth in Scotland is considered proved when a woman conceals her state of pregnancy up to within some months or weeks of her confinement. Suspicious of foul play, the law at once takes the woman under its protection, and keeps a careful watch over her until she is confined, at the same time affording every medical and other assistance the case demands. Give to the Coroner's Court power to proceed in cases of concealment of birth as well as in charges of infanticide, and let such prosecutions be based upon a more defined law, such as exists in Scotland, thereby preventing crime and saving a large population, that under our present system perish like an ephemeral race, or close a diurnal existence like the flowers of the forest, unheeded and uncared for by thoughtless humanity.

Then there is the law ruling verdicts in cases of suicide. The jury are bound to record the state of the deceased's mind at the time he committed the act. How can such a question be solved over the dead, when, while life existed, it would have puzzled the most eminent medical men to decide the point? Ay, out of twelve doctors six would have decided for sanity; six, on the contrary, for insanity. Most people will say the act is one of insanity. Be it so; but leave the solution of the question to the Almighty, and let man be content to know whether the awful deed has been committed by the unfortunate deceased, or has been the act of any one else.

While preparing a new code for the ruling of the Coroner's Court in those districts of the United Kingdom where this office holds its prerogative, the desirability of extending the Coroner's system to Scotland deserves consideration. Would not such a tribunal prove much more searching, and be hailed as a more impartial and liberal institution, than the private inquiries conducted, as at the present time in that country, by procurator fiscals?

HEADS

OF PROPOSED NEW BILL TO BE KNOWN AS
THE CORONER'S ACT.

THE PREAMBLE SETS FORTH,—All previous Acts or portions of Acts, respecting the duties and emoluments of Coroners and their Officers, or referring thereto, shall, after the passing of this Act, be repealed, as it is indispensably necessary for the better guidance of Coroners and their officers that their duties and functions shall be revised, remodelled, and strengthened, and that an addition shall be made to such duties as the passing of new Acts, and the amendment of the laws of the land since the establishment of the Coroner's Court shall demand and the ends of justice require, and it is at the same time essentially necessary that such duties and functions should be more clearly defined.

THE CLAUSES THEN PROVIDE FOR ;—

The election of Coroner by the public voice, viz., by the votes of those named on the County and Borough Parliamentary Registers, the voting not being confined to freeholders alone, but every duly qualified registered person having a vote.

The appointment of competent Deputy Coroners in districts where the duties are large and extended.

The fixing of Coroners' Salaries upon a triennial average; the duties imposed during the three years preceding the passing of the Act being taken in the first place as a basis. A Triennial Revision to take place, and an increase or decrease of salary allowable if a marked increase or decrease of duties can be proved.

The special definition of Coroners' duties and the prevention of magisterial interference.

The holding of a Magisterial Inquiry upon a Special Warrant from the Lord Chief Justice (Chief Coroner of England) should the Coroner's decision be appealed against as unsatisfactory—this only to affect cases of alleged murder or manslaughter in which no commitment has taken place by the Coroner.

The assistance and co-operation of the police, when required by the Coroners, in aiding the arrest of accused persons, and their production before the Coroner's Court.

The special definition of cases of death in which inquests shall be rendered indispensably necessary.

The performance of *post mortem* examinations and chemical analyses.

The arrest of parties on suspicion; the same powers given to Coroners in such cases as now held by police magistrates.

The fining for culpable neglect not amounting to criminal carelessness.

The restricting of apothecaries, chemists, and vendors of medicinal drugs, compounds, and poisons.

The fining for reckless dispensing, and the indiscriminate and careless sale of poisons, as also for the sale of unwholesome and impure medicinal drugs and compounds.

The payment of the Coroner for this extra duty and the Jurors summoned to receive a fee. An appeal to a superior court permitted in such cases.

The prosecution of parties at the Quarter Sessions of the Peace for the County if reckless dispensing and the sale of unwholesome and impure drugs continued after the first inquiry, and powers vested in the bench for the infliction of fine with imprisonment if necessary. An appeal to a superior court allowed.

The attendance of a public prosecutor on such occasions.

The attendance of legal representatives on behalf of accused parties.

The holding of investigations in all cases of arson, or suspected arson, although life may not have been sacrificed.

The arrest of parties on suspicion in such cases.

The holding of investigations into sanatory matters, such as where existing nuisances, bad drainage, unwholesome trades, &c., are alleged to be injurious to the public health.

The issuing of orders for the abatement of dangerous nuisances or existing sanatory evils, and the removal of unwholesome trades, &c., from towns and populous districts.

The prosecution of culpable parties at the Quarter Sessions if the nuisances, &c., remained unabated after the issuing of special orders thereon by the Court.

The indictment of culpable parties on the charge of *wilful murder* or *manslaughter* according to the weight of their culpability and the neglect and indifference displayed if death arose from existing nuisances, unwholesome trades, bad drainage, &c., for which they were responsible, whether the so inculpated parties were Government officials, local authorities, district medical officers of health, inspectors of nuisances, or the owners of the property where the fatal nuisances so existed.*

The criminal culpability of parochial officers and others concerned in the administration of relief to the poor when death arose from their neglect, indifference, or harsh conduct.

The holding of investigations in cases of alleged adulteration of food and the prosecution of culpable parties thereon.

The defining of verdicts of Coroners' Juries. The introduction of the verdict of " Not Proven " in doubtful cases of alleged criminal homicide.

The abolition of the inquiry into the state of the mind of persons who had committed suicide ; the inquiry being confined to the production of proof as to the act being suicidal or that of another.

The committal of accused parties upon the decision of a jury and the power to bail allowed at the discretion of the Coroner.

The attendance of a public prosecutor on all occasions of prosecuting at the County Assizes or Quarter Sessions.

The holding of inquiries in cases of concealment of birth. Definition of concealment of birth.

The prohibition of medical certificates where the precise cause of death is not known.

The other clauses of the Bill consist of matters of detail and routine which it is unnecessary to give in this abbreviated sketch of its general bearing. It may, however, be essential to explain that provision is particularly made for preventing that dangerous system of granting medical certificates where the precise cause of death is unknown, the restricting of Registrars of Deaths under such circumstances, and the complete remodelling of the registration system which, under existing circumstances, is no protection whatever to life. Provision is also made for the appointment of public prosecutors and public analytical officers, the division of counties and districts where the duties are too onerous for one Coroner, the restriction of voting to each particular division or district, and the auditing of Coroners' accounts for witnesses' fees and other expenses incurred. The Coroner's jurisdiction is to be alone interfered with by the Lord Chief Justice ; and Coroners will be liable to severe penalties for neglect of duty. The Act is to extend over the United Kingdom—to England and Wales, Scotland, and Ireland.

* See page 37.

EXTRACTS

FROM THE

PUBLIC PRESS.

ABRIDGED FROM "THE MORNING CHRONICLE."

A VERY important subject has been conspicuously brought under the notice of the public in a pamphlet from the pen of a member of the Metropolitan Press, the writer treating on the powers and jurisdiction of the Coroner's Court, and his object being to establish that ancient and exceedingly valuable institution on a more liberal, broad, and firmer basis than it can boast of at present, while at the same time he proposes to check the many abuses that have crept into the coroner's system, to extend the usefulness of the Court, and prevent in future any of those unseemly jarring strifes which have unfortunately so frequently taken place between coroners and magistrates in the discharge of their respective duties.

The author of this little treatise, Mr. Dempsy, is evidently well versed in the subject he writes upon, and, aided by the clear discrimination and shrewd legal acumen of Lord Brougham and the members of the Law Amendment Society, to whom the pamphlet is dedicated, it is confidently expected that a searching reform will be the result of this agitation.

While thus revising the duties of the Coroner's Court, and urging suggestions for enlarging its usefulness, Mr. Dempsy would give to the Coroner the power of arrest and remand in suspicious cases. At present he holds no power for arresting, until a jury have arrived at their decision, and while the investigation in a case of murder is proceeding the guilty may make their escape. He condemns the present addenda system, as adopted by Coroners' juries, and shows them to be illegal, by quoting such legal authorities as Lord Chief Justice Denman and Sir J. Jervis. He would have Coroners' juries confine their decisions to "aye," "nay," or "not proven," in suspicious and unsatisfactory cases. A check, he contends, is called for on the present absurd registration system. At present a registrar registers any death reported to him, the party is buried on his certificate, and the system is no protection whatever to life. A medical attendant should not be allowed to certify unless he knew the precise cause of death, and no registrar, under the pain of severe fine and dismissal from office, should be allowed to register unless on the certificate of a fully qualified medical man, who should state how long he attended the deceased before demise, and the precise cause of death.

Mr. Dempsy makes some pertinent remarks respecting the organization of the Coroner's jury, and points to the necessity for the appointment of public prosecutors, as also to the justice of allowing legal advisers to attend and speak for accused parties before the Court, such being, under the present mode, a favour depending upon the whim of the Coroner.

Abridged from "The Globe."

Amongst our most useful tribunals we must reckon that which is unprovided with any stated court—the Coroner's Inquest ; and there are few of our tribunals which we should be more sorry to lose. The tribunal is not modern. A recent writer (Mr. J. J. Dempsy) traces it to the reign of Alfred the Great, just as Virgil traces the birth of his patron to the traditional founder of Rome, the pious Prince of Troy. These traditional origins for institutions form one proof of the esteem in which they have been held for a long series of ages. Curiously enough, the value of the English Coroner's Court has been illustrated by the want of a similar tribunal in Scotland.

Mr. Dempsy recommends that the Coroner should have a seat on the County Bench, and that he should hold his court in some established building—the district police court, the vestry hall, or parochial offices, at times when these buildings were not needed for other purposes. Our author also proposes a much more regular holding of inquests in cases of violence, alleged violence, accident, arson, and many other doubtful circumstances ; the enforcement of all fines for the non-attendance of jurors ; and a larger power in the Coroner of inflicting fines for cases of *culpable* neglect or criminal carelessness, a species of retributive penalty now only obtained through some circuitous action at law, sometimes founded on fiction, such as "loss of service," &c. Mr. Dempsy proposes that the Coroner should have a Deputy, with a stated salary ; and that there should be appointed for his Court a public prosecutor, charged with the preliminary inquiries into cases of murder, arson, negligence, &c. In British India a medical officer is retained to examine the body and to assist the Court ; a great improvement on our English system, which treats the medical witness with mistrust and injuriously restricts his functions. There is no doubt that the exertions of a public prosecutor would sometimes bring to bear evidence that at present lapses for want of concentrated attention, and he would be very useful in instituting proceedings against responsible public officers where their negligence resulted in fatal injury to health.

Abridged from "The Daily Telegraph."

It is not difficult to perceive that the Coroner, so far as relates to the magistrates, is placed in a false position. Being remunerated by fees, and the amount of his emoluments depending consequently upon the inquests he may be required to hold, it is at his own peril if he institutes inquiries which a county bench may consider unnecessary. Who ought to be considered the proper judge on this point—the man who has been selected from his medical or legal acquirements specially to perform this duty, or an irresponsible and arbitrary body, who care much more, in all probability, for keeping down the rates than for doubtful deaths being investigated ? In truth, now that a conflict of authority is liable to lead to unseemly disputes, and that a Coroner is apt to be regarded by a magistrate, whether rural or stipendiary, as a very superfluous sort of personage, it is time that the office should be remodelled, its functions and responsibilities distinctly defined, and such amendments made as altered circumstances may have rendered necessary. On this subject we have a pamphlet before us by Mr. J. J. Dempsy, who has not only pointed out many anomalies requiring removal, but made some useful suggestions of reform. He justly considers that the Coroner's office is not one that ought to be restricted or superseded by any other authority, but that, being a people's Court, and having charge of matters affecting life and death, its powers ought to be enlarged, well-defined, and independent of magisterial interference. The manifest object of the magnates at quarter sessions is to limit the powers of the Coroner to cases of suicide, sudden death, or evident murder ; whereas, the principle rightly laid down by Mr. Dempsy is, that not only deaths enveloped in mystery and suspicion, but *every* case where the cause of death is unknown, should be the subject of investigation. The knowledge that such inquiries would take place must of itself tend powerfully to the repression of crime, and even the intending secret murderer might hesitate to carry out his fell purpose, if fully conscious that the peril of a rigid inquiry would be incurred.

There are two points in connexion with the present system that seem especially objectionable : one is, the payment of the Coroner by fees, according to the work done ; and another, the power given to the magistrates to dispute and disallow the sums charged, according to their view of the necessity of such inquests being held. If the object be to degrade the Coroner, this doubtless is the right way to do it. A better mode of upholding his dignity and ensuring his usefulness would be by the payment of an annual salary, which would at once obviate the temptation of instituting inquiries without adequate cause, and free him from the trammels of magisterial interference. It is also satisfactorily shown that the Coroner's jurisdiction might be beneficially extended in those cases in which death has occurred through the callous indifference, neglect, or cruelty of parish officials, in refusing to relieve the poor and destitute. The practice of giving medical certificates, without adequate knowledge of the cause of death, is too important to be passed over, since it is one that may be employed for the worst purposes. The main object, however, in the various changes that may be considered needful, is to give full power to the Coroner, in all cases of death demanding a legal inquiry; and this can only be done by his emancipation from magisterial thraldom and interference, which now threaten to destroy the usefulness and dignity of one of the best and most ancient of our social institutions.

From "The Western Flying Post."

Public attention has lately been specially called to the proceedings connected with Coroners' Courts, and the most unseemly legal differences which have arisen between the magisterial bench and the Coroner's Court, in regard to what is or is not necessary to be done before a Coroner should hold an inquest, and make his charge for the same. It would be a work of supererogation in this day to point out the necessity, usefulness, and power of such a Court as that of Coroners. The great alterations made of late years in our system of police, and the distinctive appointments of county and borough magistrates, call for some more specific rules, in order to the due administration of affairs in both Courts, so that the power and dignity of each may be supported. Mr. Dempsy, in the pamphlet before us, has endeavoured to show how this desirable end might be effected. We quite agree with him that the importance and usefulness of the Coroner's Court cannot be too highly rated. Its popular constitution as a "People's Court," and its being presided over by gentlemen of legal acumen, strongly recommend it to public approval. It is a shield against oppression ; it looks after the physical condition of the community ; it stirs up careless officials with regard to public nuisances, and seldom fails to bring home to the right persons, by a chain of circumstantial local evidence, the deliberate murders of those whose diabolical deeds were, as they thought, perpetrated with unfathomable secrecy and impossibility of proof. These are some of the benefits of this democratic institution. We should therefore look with no small degree of suspicion at any attempt to destroy or impair its due administration. Our space will not permit us to follow Mr. Dempsy through all his arguments against the evil which would follow any attempt made to abolish the Coroner's Court. To some of those arguments we feel disposed to demur ; but in their main points we cordially agree.

From "The Morning Chronicle."

The public remember the dark deeds of Palmer, and think of them with horror, but such appears not to be the case with the magistrates of Staffordshire, where this notorious criminal flourished and carried on, without check, hindrance, or fear of discovery, his villanous and murderous designs ; for within the last few days that sapient body are to be found in Quarter Sessions assembled doing their best to throw open the gates to a repetition of such atrocious crimes, by scandalously usurping the Coroner's rights, and making that ancient and important office—that only protection for human life against such assassins as a Palmer—a mere tribunal in name and a nothing in its administration. Indeed, the magistrates of Staffordshire appear to do all in their power to degrade the office of Coroner, to deride its august and important functions, and to reduce it to a simple question of pounds, shillings, and pence.

It is with pain we observe at the last Staffordshire Quarter Sessions the magistrates adopt such a course as this, and in priding themselves upon a diminution of county expenditure do so at the expense and degradation of the Coroners, whose expenses—be it remarked out of pocket—they disallow after those gentlemen have performed most zealously and efficiently their onerous and at the same time highly important duties. Notwithstanding the Coroner's fees and expenses are reduced for the past quarter to the extent of 151*l.* 16*s.* 2*d.*, yet the magistrates are to be found cutting off those expenses which the Coroners have incurred, and previously paid out of their own pockets.

Now, by what right or on what plea of justice or fair play can the magistrates so act ?   The Coroners have felt themselves in the efficient discharge of their duties called upon to hold certain inquiries ; ay, more, by Act of Parliament, they are bound to hold such investigations when called upon, they have in all probability been put to much expense in proceeding to some distant part of a district, and yet, after being some months out of pocket, they are refused the necessary expenses incurred. Surely this can be neither just nor proper ; and what must be the lamentable result ?   Coroners will be apt to be backward in holding inquiries, crime of the worst magnitude—secret crime—that which Alfred the Great wished by the formation of this institution to suppress, will spring up, and Palmers will revel in their poisonous machinations.

The Coroners have the most weighty duties to perform in protecting the public health and preserving human life.   They are either honourable and trustworthy men, and men fitted to discharge the high functions of their office, or they are not. Let the country decide the merits of their case, but do not let a body of magistrates take upon themselves, for the sake of the saving of a few paltry pounds, to degrade the office by dubbing its ministers as little better than extortioners, and trampling upon the rights and authority of the Crown officers.

It is really a pity that the magistrates of Staffordshire do not view things in this light, after the sad details of the Palmer tragedy.   Palmer was no doubt well aware of the check kept on Coroners in Staffordshire, and the few inquests held, and that post-mortem examinations were very rare, even in the most mysterious cases, and therefore every temptation was open to him to commit his heinous crimes ; while, at the same time, a knowledge of the searching character of the Coroner's Court, when properly carried out, and a dread of post-mortem examinations, might have checked him, coward as he was, in his terrible designs.

The magistrates in this and other counties should bear in mind that prevention is better than cure ; but it is to be feared that such suggestions have no avail with the bench, so that the only hope that can be held out is that the Legislature will, ere long, throw a protection around the Coroner, and prevent his duties being trifled with and really trampled upon.

From "The Durham County Advertiser."

Between bodies of men such as the magistracy and the Coroners of this country, both occupying dignified positions, both discharging difficult and delicate functions, it is a serious misfortune that any difference of feeling or opinion should arise. Such differences, however, have recently arisen in various parts of the country, and, if not removed by still higher authorities, threaten evil consequences both to law and humanity. We read of "unseemly bickerings" in West Kent, in Gloucestershire, in Warwickshire, and, by a report in our own columns of last week, it is shown that the evil is at our own doors. We refer to the late magisterial examination of Coroners' accounts for the four divisions of this county, during a great portion of which there occurred—we will not use the words "unseemly bickerings"—words somewhat disrespectful, but, certainly, disputes of rather a painful nature. On one side, indeed, there was absolute power to over-rule—the other having no power of appeal; but the over-ruling was manifestly regarded as harsh by the over-ruled; and the submission of the latter, just as manifestly, looked a little ungracious and unwilling.

In the meantime, is it not degrading to the old and honourable office of Coroner, that such disputes should exist? Every Coroner is understood to be a gentleman, a person of education, attainments, position, and repute. He is expected to know something of law, surgery, medical jurisprudence; to exert some of the keenest faculties and best properties of our nature; to be shrewd, impartial, disinterested; to detect and rivet the first links of evidence against probable guilt; to take the first steps in the path of public justice. Yet, very frequently it is not till the close of a well-conducted inquest that a single link can be traced, or a single step determined; that the question of suspicion or non-suspicion—of violence accidental, or guilty,—can possibly be answered. Surely, it is wrong that individuals holding such an office should be subject to such aggrievement and degradation; should be driven to sue and plead, as it were, for a petty remuneration for honourably discharged duties. We say "petty," for, at the utmost, what is this remuneration? In 1856, all the Coroners of England and Wales put together received less than 30,000*l.*, or rather less than an average of 90*l.* each; out of which came the salaries of their deputies and clerks, the expenses of juries and witnesses.

One thing, indeed, is offered them as an alternative, or compromise—payment of expenses for inquests they do not hold—after previous examination as to the necessity for any inquest.

But, let them travel whatever distance, endure whatever fatigue and disgust—and really hold an inquest, which is objected to finally by the magistrates—not a penny either of fee or expenses will be theirs. Duty must be its own reward. Would not the tithe of all this prove that Coroners should be remunerated by fixed salaries, and not by disputable fee for disputable duties? Let the labourer and his hire be worthy of each other.

Macintosh, Printer, Great New-street, London.